SWIFTEST

GOOD TRY!

BEST FOOTWORK

TEAMWORK AWARD

BEST EFFORT

Finklehopper Frog Cheers

Irene Livingston   Illustrations by Brian Lies

Tricycle Press
Berkeley · Toronto

Finklehopper, Finklehopper,
Finklehopper Frog,
hadn't felt so happy
since he was a pollywog!

There was going to be a picnic—
oh, a fabuloso one—

down beside the water
in the sparkle of the sun.

But Fink began to worry,
his excitement falling flat.

"They'll laugh at me or try to grab my groovy pork-pie hat!"

"Aw, Ruby Rabbit's going, too.
I guess I'll be okay.

"So even though I'm scared to go,
I'll do it anyway."

Along came Itchy Flea who howled,
"Hey, where'd ya get the hat!"

And Yowlereen said, "Hi there, frog.
Who let you out in **that?**"

So Ruby smiled and winked, "Hey, cat, you're lookin' fine today!
And, Itchy, thanks, you like the hat!"

The bullies slunk away.

Finklehopper chuckled, "Rube,
you really chased those chumps.
And just with words, I'm pleased to say,
instead of thumps and bumps."

"Oh, Finklehopper, Finklehopper, Finklehopper Frog,

let's find the hopping track. Forget
that yappin' cat and dog."

But when they reached the track
the race was just about to start.
Then Ruby saw a crushing sight
that almost broke her heart.

Sue Kangaroo was in the race!
And Ruby wailed, "Oh, no!
She's bound to beat me. **Holy cow,**

that kangaroo can go!"

"Come on! You're like a rocket, Rube,
my lightning-footed friend.
You'll knock 'em cold, you'll hop so fast.
You'll wow them in the end!"

So Ruby's heart was hopeful,
as the crowd so tensely stood.

They hollered, "Go!" and off she sped,
just like she knew she could.

The crowd went bonkers,

bellowed,

brayed,

and Finkle cheered, "Yahoo!"

With one last flying, smoking burst

she came in...

...number two.

Her tears began a-raining.
There was thunder in her face.
"No fair!" she cried in stormy grief,
"I should have won that race!"

"Oh, Ruby Rabbit!" Finkle said,
"We know what you can do!

You do your awesome, flat-out best.
For that I'm proud of you!

"Plus you were worried, just like me,
but did it anyway.

See, when you go ahead and try
your worries never stay."

"Poor Sue! She won but feels so bad
to see you all upset.
Now dry your tears, my dripping pal.
You're getting me all wet!"

So Ruby thought a sec and said,
"I think I understand."

She turned. "Congratulations Sue!
Here, let me shake your hand."

"Well thanks," said Sue the Kangaroo.
Good sports are great to see.

"And yOU were rollin' too out there,
ka-boing-ing after me."

"Now, Rube!" said Fink, "It's time to eat!
I'm sniffing deviled egg.
There's hot dogs, pizza, ice cream, too.
Wooo-eee! Let's shake a leg!"

So off they hopped. "Oh Fink!" said Rube.
"You really clued me in.
We do our best and **that's** the way. . .

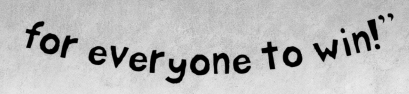

for everyone to win!"

For Connor Dykstra.

With thanks to Margret Vasarhelyi and Heather Scoular.—I.L.

For Wende and Harry Devlin, whose books started it all for me.—B.L.

Text copyright © 2005 by Irene Livingston
Illustrations copyright © 2005 by Brian Lies

Tricycle Press
a little division of Ten Speed Press
P.O. Box 7123
Berkeley, California 94707
www.tenspeed.com

Design by Tasha Hall
Typeset in FF Bokka
The illustrations in this book were rendered in acrylic paint.

Library of Congress Cataloging-in-Publication Data

Livingston, Irene, 1932-
Finklehopper Frog cheers / Irene Livingston ; illustrations by Brian Lies.
     p. cm.
Summary: When Finklehopper Frog and Ruby Rabbit go to a picnic, their friendship helps them
weather some challenges and disappointments.
ISBN 1-58246-138-4
[1. Self-esteem—Fiction. 2. Friendship—Fiction. 3. Picnicking—Fiction. 4. Frogs—Fiction.
5. Rabbits—Fiction. 6. Animals—Fiction. 7. Stories in rhyme.] I. Lies, Brian, ill. II. Title.
PZ8.3+
[E]—dc22

2004016104

First printing, 2005
Printed in China

JUNE 1, 200

WLS
FFLED

DOVE
DEPR

GOOD SPORTS, GREAT PICNIC!
A FUN TIME IS HAD BY ALL
BY ANNE HINGA